10

Little Hermit Crabs

Hermit crabs don't make shells of their own. They live in second-hand shells made by other creatures. When a hermit crab grows too big for its shell, it finds a new one and moves in. Hermit crabs are named after hermits - people who like to live alone, sometimes in small caves. But hermit crabs don't like to be alone. In the wild they live in colonies of 100 or more.

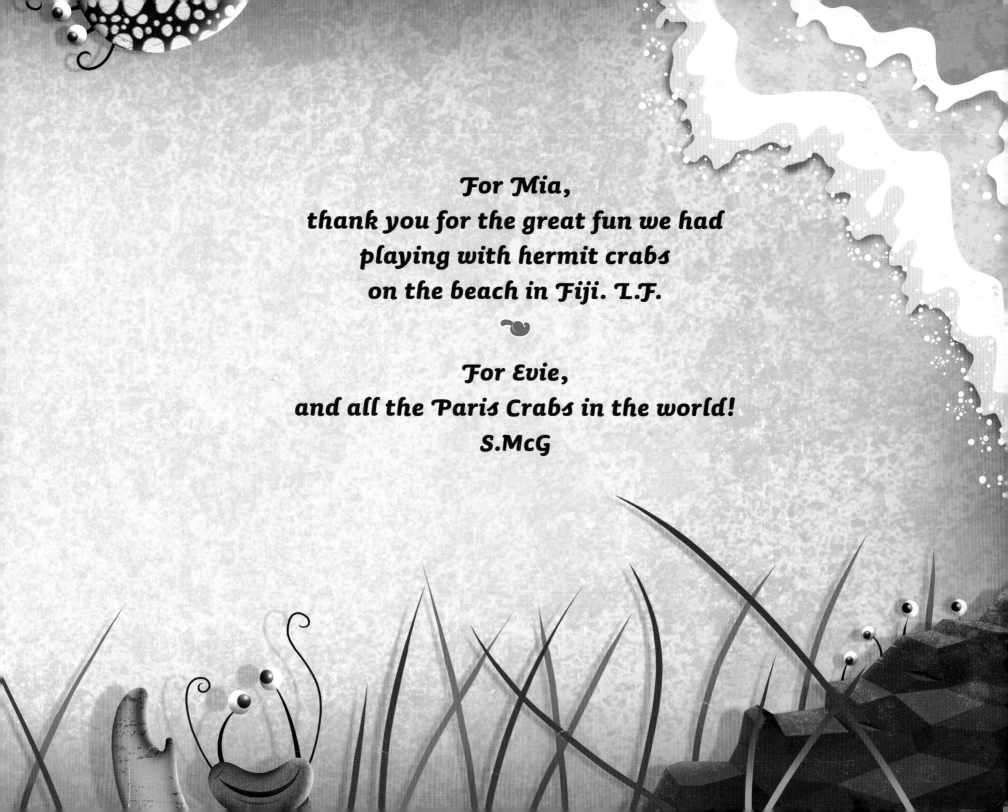

For Mia,
thank you for the great fun we had
playing with hermit crabs
on the beach in Fiji. L.F.

For Evie,
and all the Paris Crabs in the world!
S.McG

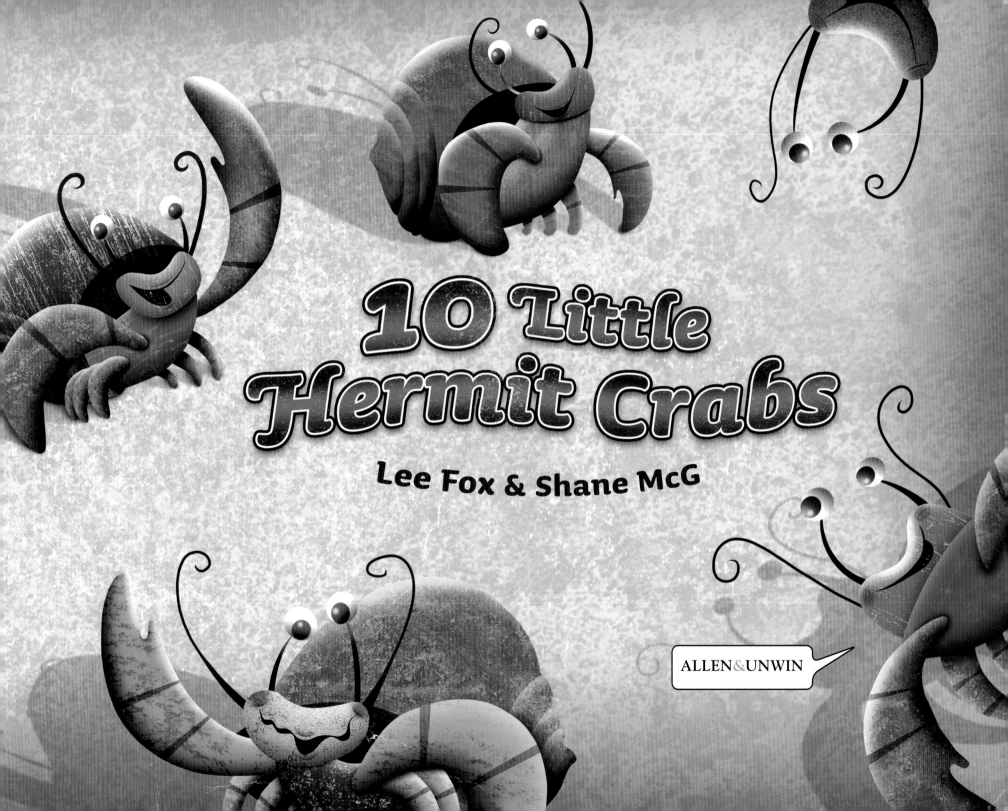

10 Little Hermit Crabs

Lee Fox & Shane McG

ALLEN&UNWIN

10 little hermit crabs
scuttle to the beach.
Down swoops a seagull.
Screech!

Screech!

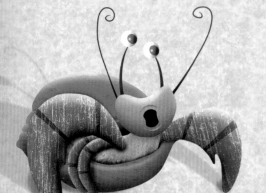

Scree

Hush, says the seashore.

Shh, says the sea.

ch!

How many hermit crabs will there be?

9 little hermit crabs scurry on with speed.
One gets **tangled** in a pile of seaweed.

Hush, says the seashore. Shh, says the sea.
How many hermit crabs will there be?

8 little hermit crabs
share a shady spot.
One crab's
trapped
in a crayfish pot.

Hush, says the seashore.
Shh, says the sea.
How many hermit crabs
will there be?

7 little hermit crabs **snaffle** six new shells.
One poor crab has **nowhere** to dwell.

6 little hermit crabs

scamper in a throng.

One stops to listen

to a dolphin's song.

Hush, says the seashore. Shh, says the sea. How many hermit crabs will there be?

5 little hermit crabs burrow underground.
One crab's **buried** by a big sandy mound.

Hush, says the seashore. Shh, says the sea.
How many hermit crabs will there be?

4 little hermit crabs
sprint along the sand.

One's plucked up by a child's small hand.

Hush, says the seashore.
Shh, says the sea.
How many hermit crabs will there be?

3 little hermit crabs frolic and paddle.

One meets a **Shark,** and the other two skedaddle!

Hush, says the seashore.
Shh, says the sea.

How many hermit crabs will there be?

2 little hermit crabs scramble, claw and climb.

One gets **hooked** on a fisherman's line.

Hush, says the seashore. Shh, says the sea.
How many hermit crabs will there be?

1 little hermit crab *alone* on the pier...

9 little hermit crabs shout,

"We're over

here!'

Hush, says the seashore. Shh, says the sea.
How many hermit crabs will there be?

10 little hermit crabs **waving** at me.